Letters to Anyone
and Everyone

Letters to Anyone and Everyone

STORIES BY

Toon Tellegen

ILLUSTRATED BY

Jessica Ahlberg

TRANSLATED BY

Martin Cleaver

BOXER BOOKS

Introduction

Toon Tellegen first began to
invent animal stories to tell his
daughter at bedtime. Then, when
his daughter grew older, he decided
to write them down. He created a
world where there is only one forest,
one river, one ocean, and one oak
tree; a world of imagination where
anything is possible. Toon has been
writing stories about the squirrel,
the ant, and the other animals in the

forest for over 25 years, and to date
more than 300 of them have been
published in his native Holland.
His work has been translated
into many different languages
and enjoyed by children all over
the world. *Letters to Anyone and
Everyone*, and its companion, *The
Squirrel's Birthday and Other Parties*,
are the first titles in a new series.

Contents

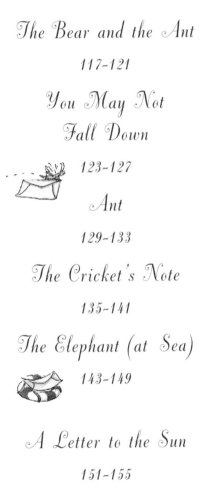

Dear Snail

Dear Snail,

May I invite you to dance with me on top of your house? Just a few steps? That's what I want most of all.

I promise I'll dance very delicately, so we won't fall through your roof.

But of course, you can never be really sure.

The elephant

Dear Elephant,

Thank you for your letter.

I'm certain I'd like to dance
with you on my roof one day.
I'm almost convinced of that.
I think I'm a very good dancer.
But unfortunately I don't think
it's such a good idea just
at the moment.

The snail

One Winter's Day

One winter's day,
the squirrel wrote
a letter to the ant:

Dear Ant,

    Ant Ant Ant

    Ant Ant Ant

    Ant Ant Ant.

    Dear Ant

    Ant Ant Ant

    Ant.

    Dear Ant.

    Dear Ant.

    Ant.

    The squirrel

14

It was a strange letter and the squirrel didn't really know why he'd written it. But he dressed it in a hat and coat because it was chilly, explained which way to go, and opened the door.

The letter stepped outside cautiously, climbed down the beech tree, walked through the snow, and tapped on the ant's window.

"Who's there?" asked the ant.

"The letter," said the letter.

"The letter?" the ant replied, and he opened the door in surprise.

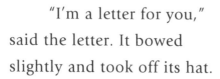

"I'm a letter for you,"
said the letter. It bowed
slightly and took off its hat.

The ant studied the letter from all
sides, then opened it cautiously.

"I think I'll read you," he said.

"That's fine," said the letter.

When the ant had finished reading,
he rubbed his hands together and

said, "Do sit down,
letter, sit down.
What would
you like?"

"Well," said the letter hesitantly,

"I don't really know."

"Something sweet?" the ant asked.

"That's a good idea!" said the letter,
rustling with pleasure.

The ant took his pen and wrote
something sweet at the top of the
letter. He stopped and thought
before writing *something warm*
at the bottom. Then he ate some
honey. The letter and the ant sat
together for a long time.
Occasionally the ant stood up and
wrote something in the letter's margin.
When darkness fell, the letter said
goodbye. Snow was falling as it
waded slowly toward the
beech tree. When it got there,
it climbed up the trunk and
slid itself under the
squirrel's door.

"Well I never," said the squirrel. "You came back."

"Yes," said the letter, and it told the squirrel all about what had happened on its visit to the ant.

"Do you know what the ant thinks about you, Squirrel?" asked the letter.

"What does he think?" said the squirrel.

"Just read me," said the letter.

The squirrel read, and when he'd finished, he asked the letter if he could put it under his pillow.

"Of course," said the letter.

The squirrel's house creaked as the storm raged outside.

The snowflakes
got bigger
and the world
became whiter
and whiter.

But the squirrel
and the letter noticed
nothing of that.
They slept and
dreamed of words
and sweet ink.

To the Stranger Who
Crosses The Water

$\mathcal{D}$ear Stranger,

The salmon told me that you exist.
He says you're real. But he doesn't
know what you look like and he doesn't
know what plans you have for the water.

I'm the carp.

Maybe you know me. Perhaps you
even came to my birthday party. There
were many animals there, so I can't be
sure. If you came to my birthday party,
you may have heard me recite something.
Or had you already left by then?

If you were still there, did you think it was nice?

I'm writing to tell you that I am very happy with the water.

If you're responsible, then thank you.

I think it could flow a little faster sometimes, with bubbles in it and little eddies. I just love eddies. Little eddies, that is. Could you provide some?

You could also give me an occasional flood. It's so wonderful to swim up a tree. If only you knew, you'd make sure it kept flooding.

Maybe you do know, but it isn't easy,
all that flooding. I also know things
that aren't easy but I still want to do them.
Jumping, for example. Jumping in the air.
I wonder if you can do that. Maybe you
know a good way. If you do, I'd love to
hear it from you.

But that big freeze-up in the winter;
why do you do that? What's the point?
Please don't!

The carp stopped writing for a bit
and thought. Then he carried on:

I do apologize if I got carried away there.

But have you ever been frozen in the water? It's terrible!

Now I'm going to go and have another swim.

By the way, you don't have to remain anonymous. You could just reveal your identity to me, if you prefer. I can keep my mouth shut; you can count on that. But of course, you can remain anonymous if you like.

Would you mind if I say goodbye now? Goodbye.

The carp

The Ant's Journey

$\mathcal{S}$quirrel,

I'm leaving and I'm never coming back. Of course you think, "Yes, that's what he always says."

But this time I mean it!

I'M NEVER COMING BACK.

If you were here, you'd see how I'm writing this letter.

With great determination.

That's what they say.

With great determination, I hereby inform you that I'm leaving and never coming back.

My decision is final.

When this letter is finished, I shall leave. By the time you read this letter, I will be far away.

If you want to give me anything for my journey, now is the time. Honey or something like that. Not a big pot—I couldn't carry that. Well, perhaps if it was creamy honey. I could manage a big pot of that, because I could divide it into two smaller pots. Or a box of stewed sugar. That would be fine too. Whatever it is, it has to be sweet.

I'll drop by to pick it up before I leave. If it's too big to take with me, that won't be a problem. We can eat just as much as necessary to make it small enough to carry. Too much is fine. Too little would be far worse. What would we do then?

After that, Squirrel, after that, I really will leave.

See you later,

The ant

One Morning, Early in Summer

*O*ne morning, early in the summer, a little note blew under the squirrel's door.

> *Squirrel,*
> *I was on my way to see you.*
> *But then I got lost.*
> *The elephant*

The squirrel read the note a couple of times, thought deeply, and wrote:

> *Elephant,*
> *Where did you get lost?*
> *The squirrel*

It was a strange question, he
thought. But he had no idea what else
to write, so he sent his note anyway.

Soon, a reply arrived.

Squirrel,

In a tree.
The elephant

The squirrel read the note, then
looked out of his window. He saw
the elephant tottering at the top of
the oak tree. He wrote quickly:

Elephant,
Hang on. I'm on my way.

   The squirrel

By the time the note reached the elephant, he was halfway down the oak tree. He just had time to read it before he hit the ground with an enormous thud.

A moment later, he opened his eyes. He used his trunk to count the bumps on his head. "1, 8, 100," he counted. He felt very dazed by his fall.

He looked up to find the squirrel standing over him.

"I was on my way to see you," the elephant whispered.

"Yes," said the squirrel. He sat down beside the elephant in the grass.

"I wanted . . ."
the elephant began.
"Would you like to dance with me?"

The squirrel didn't reply.

"You don't want to?"
asked the elephant and he pressed
his face into the ground.

"Yes," said the squirrel.
"I do want to."

Then, very cautiously,
he pulled the elephant
to his feet.

They put an arm around each other's waists and began to dance.

It was more like rocking than dancing, as the elephant couldn't lift his feet off the ground. He still felt delighted though, and occasionally called out a cheerful, "Oh!"

Dear Letter

The squirrel sat at his table.
He wanted to write a letter
but he didn't know who to.
He made a start by writing:

Dear

He put down his pen and thought
hard. The wind started blowing gently.
The window was open and the blank,
white paper rustled impatiently.

"Very well, letter," thought the squirrel.

"I'll think of someone for you in a
minute. Is it possible to write a letter to
a letter?" he wondered.

It was a strange thought. It was like tapping yourself on your shoulder while you were asleep and saying,

"Squirrel . . . don't sleep."

His thoughts tripped over each other.

"According to the ant," he thought to himself, "you can write a letter to anyone, even the rain, or a heatwave, or the night."

He picked up his pen again and wrote:

Dear Letter,

I'm the squirrel. Of course, you know that. It feels very strange to be writing to you, because you get bigger as I write. And if I were to start again, you'd suddenly be very small. So I never know exactly what you're like.

The squirrel stopped writing.

"This is a very strange letter," he thought. "How should I send it? And how is the letter going to read itself? Folded up? Or smoothed out? And what about writing back? Can a letter write a letter?"

His mind began to grind.
It felt as if heavy crates were
being dragged from one side
of his head to the other.
Quickly, he signed his name at
the bottom of the letter. The wind
was blowing harder now, and
suddenly the letter to the letter
shot up in the air, flew round
briefly, then exploded.
It wasn't a loud bang, but
the squirrel nearly fell over
backward, chair and all.

Hundreds of scraps of paper fluttered down and fell on his shoulders and back and on the table, and floor. There was paper everywhere. Each piece was so small that not even one single letter fitted on it.

The squirrel nodded and thought, "That's because of me."

The wind had dropped.

"Could the letter have been angry?" wondered the squirrel. "Or did it jump to pieces from joy because someone had finally written to it?"

He stood up and paced back and forth across his room, carefully avoiding the pieces of letter that were littering the floor.

"Goodbye, letter," he said softly.

The pieces of letter rustled and moved a little. For a moment, the squirrel thought that he heard them reply, "Goodbye, Squirrel."

"That's impossible," he told himself. There are things that really are impossible. He was certain of that.

A Huge Cake

$\mathcal{D}$ear Squirrel,

On your birthday, there's sure to be
a huge cake. Just this once, could I
eat the cake all on my own?

Preferably a honey cake.

Everyone can watch.

I'll eat it more beautifully and greedily
than has ever been seen before.

Everyone will clap and cheer,
I promise you.

Then everything can carry on as
before (best wishes, unwrapping presents,
dancing, saying farewell, saying it was so
much fun, asking who's going to have
a birthday soon, etc.).

It's only a wish, Squirrel.

The bear

Dear Bear,

That's fine. I'll make two cakes, instead of just one.

The squirrel

Dear Squirrel,

Thank you for your letter. When I've started eating and everyone is clapping and cheering, would you mind if I carry on and eat the other cake as well?

Everyone will jump in the air with admiration for me, I'm sure of it. They'll quack and whistle and hiss. Then it really will be an unforgettable birthday. But if you made three cakes, that would be perfect. I'm sure of that, Squirrel. Three large cakes. And if they're all honey cakes, then four.

The bear

49

The Mole's Letters

$\mathcal{L}$etters? Me? I never get letters," thought the mole. He dug a tunnel through the dark earth, feeling sorry for himself.

"Not even a greeting, or anything like that," he thought.

"Or an invitation to a party in the desert, or under the ice. Never."

He thumped angrily on the ground, but there was no answer.

"There's only one person who wants to write to me," he thought, "and that's me."

And so, in the darkness, deep underground, he wrote himself letters, one after the other:

Dear Mole,
Yours sincerely,
The mole

or

Dear Mole,
I miss you.
The mole

Once he'd finished writing
each letter, he hid it somewhere
under the mud.

Then, a little later, he would
chance upon it and read it.
Sometimes the letters
brought tears
to his eyes.

"Thank you very much, Mole,"
he thought. Or, "I miss you too, Mole."
Sometimes he threw a party for all
the senders of all his letters. Then he
ran from one side to the other of the
darkest of all his tunnels and
caverns. He danced too.
"Am I really happy?"
he wondered as he danced
with himself. At the end of one
of these parties, he went and sat
in a corner and wrote a letter to
himself, with the immortal words:

Dear Mole
You have to go on a journey.
The mole.

He nodded and went on a journey.
Up he climbed, toward the
mysterious air. He held his breath,
saw the light shining down
through the earth, and slowly
climbed on.

That evening, he paid an
unexpected visit to the squirrel.
They drank tea while the mole
talked about his parties deep under
the ground; large, dark parties
without a trace of light.

The squirrel shook his head in
amazement. The mole stirred his
tea and hoped that time would
now finally stand still.

The Elephant Note

One day, early in
winter, the elephant
paid a visit to the squirrel.
When he arrived at the squirrel's house,
he swung back and forth on the lamp,
fell a few times, and stood up again.
Then he sat by the half of the table that
was still standing and drank a cup of
willow tea. The squirrel sat on a chair
leg and licked a sweet beechnut. They
remained silent for a long time.

"We're really happy now, aren't we?" said the elephant. The squirrel nodded.

Suddenly a dark look clouded the elephant's face.

"I have to be going," he said.

"Yes," said the squirrel.

There was a brief silence.

"I fear," said the elephant, "that I'm going to fall down again."

The squirrel said nothing. He couldn't remember the elephant ever going home any other way.

"I don't want to fall down any more!" exclaimed the elephant. He broke the half table and his cup with his front right foot.

He sat down on the
ground somberly.
"I just keep falling.
All the time!" he said.

The squirrel was
eager to help
him and
thought deeply.

"What if I send you?" he said.

"Send me?"

"As a note."

"As a note?"
said the elephant.

The squirrel had already
grabbed his pen. He wrote

in large letters on the elephant's belly:

Dear Elephant,
How are you getting on?

He stopped writing for a moment.
"What's this all about?" he thought
to himself. "I know very well how he's
getting on."

He scratched out *How are you getting*
on?
"Ouch!" the elephant said.
Have a nice trip, wrote the squirrel
in meticulous lettering.

"That's all you need," he thought.

He wrote his name gently under
the letter, not far from the elephant's
navel. The elephant tried to read what
had been written on his belly, but the
squirrel opened the door
and pushed him outside.

61

"Wow!" called the elephant.

The wind caught him and blew him away.

"Bye, Elephant," called the squirrel. "See you soon!"

"Bye, Squirrel," called the elephant.

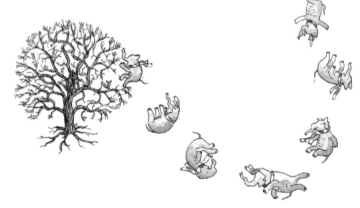

The wind blew the elephant high into the sky and over the woods, over the river, and toward his home.

Late that evening
he was delivered there.
In the middle of the night, while
the squirrel was still busy putting his
chairs and table back together, a little
note blew in under his door.

Dear Squirrel,
I blew all the way home just fine.
Thanks very much.
I'm not crumpled.
Your friend,
The note

Satisfied, the squirrel fell asleep in
what was left of his bed.

The Tortoise's Hurry

One morning, the tortoise
woke up and was horrified to discover
that he was in a hurry.

"Just a minute!" he called.
But before he could stop himself,
he was on his way. He shuffled on
at high speed and by early afternoon
he'd already gone a long way.

He moaned and sobbed
and occasionally dressed
himself down most severely, but it
didn't help. He was in a hurry.

At the end of his tether,
he wrote a letter to the snail:

Dear Snail,

I'm very sorry to say I'm in a hurry.

What should I do? Quickly!

The tortoise

In the early evening,
a slow, neatly written letter
floated down in front of the
tortoise's nose. It read:

Dearest Tortoise,

That is a tragedy for you.

It's so cruel when you're in a hurry.

Fight your way out of it and defeat it.

*Fold it up into an insignificant ball, then
bury it in the ground.*

*Above all, keep your cool. If you and
I lose our cool, what then?*

The snail

So, as calmly as he could,
the tortoise started to crumple up
the hurry he was in.

By late evening he
had finished.

He put the insignificant,
yet still rather restless crumpled
ball in the ground.

"Indeed," he thought.

"I'm not in a hurry any more."

That night he stayed where he was.
He closed his eyes and didn't even
sigh once. "Thank goodness," was
the only thing he could think.

The next day, he shuffled very
calmly back to the oak tree where
he lived.

"I suppose," he thought, "I should
thank the snail. But not too quickly.
Only after a while."

And calmly and collectedly,
he forgot that he had ever been
in a hurry.

A Black Letter

*O*ne morning in winter, the squirrel received a letter.

It was a black letter. He'd never seen a letter like this before. He frowned as he read:

This is a somber statement.
Everything is going wrong.

That's all it said. There was no mention of a sender. It didn't even say at the top that it was to the squirrel.

The squirrel sat down in his chair. He knew the wind never made a mistake when delivering letters.

He read the letter a few more times, but each time he understood it less. He put on his thick coat and went to see the ant.

It was snowing and
the woods were groaning
with frost. Shivering, the
squirrel knocked on the
ant's door and showed
him the letter.

"Yes," said the ant.
"That is a somber
statement."

"What does it mean,
'going wrong'?" asked
the squirrel.

"Going wrong . . ."
said the ant, scratching
his head. "Well . . ."
He tried to explain
to the squirrel
what "going
wrong" was.

It turned into a long and
complicated story and by the time
the ant had finished, the squirrel felt
as if he had a heavy rock pressing
down on his back. But he still had
no idea what "going wrong" was.

"Let's have something sweet to drink,"
said the ant. "While we still can."

"While we still can?" asked the squirrel
in amazement. He didn't understand what
the ant meant by that at all.

"Yes," said the ant.
"That's what they say."

"Oh," said the squirrel.

The squirrel and the ant sat in silence as they drank something sweet. Outside, the wind whistled through the trees.

As evening fell, the ant said, "You should be going, Squirrel."

"Yes," said the squirrel. He walked home through the dark woods.

"I'll go home while I still can," he thought. It was a strange, dark thought.

That evening, he sat by his window for hours. "Now I'm sure to be dejected," he thought, as he looked out into the darkness.

Late that night, his door suddenly blew open and a letter flew in. It was in an envelope that was frozen stiff and covered in snow.

The squirrel wiped the snow off the letter, tore it open, and read:

This is a cheerful statement.
Everything is going right after all.

It was a peculiar letter. The squirrel climbed on the table and said to himself, "Now I'm the elephant."

He swung back and forth on the lamp, until he and the lamp fell to the ground. "It doesn't matter, really!" he called out to everything that had broken.

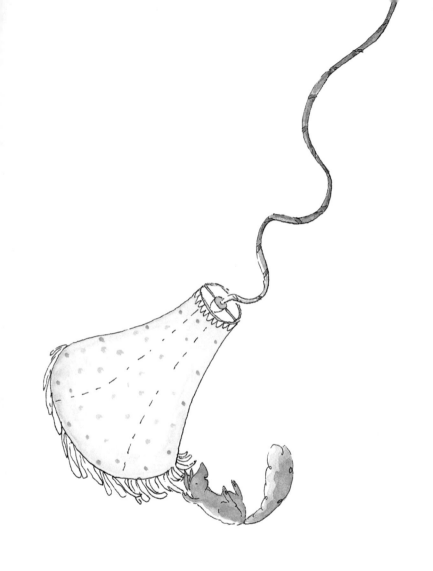

Dear Animals

$\mathcal{D}$ear Animals,

Who is celebrating their
birthday today?

If no one is, then who would
like to have an early birthday?

If no one would like that, then who
wants to celebrate something else
and invite me for cake and tart?

If no one wants to do that
either, then who wants to bake
a cake (with honey and cream
and sweet jelly and melted sugar)
and to ask me to come around
and eat it up?

If no one wants to do that,
what then?

Help me.

The bear

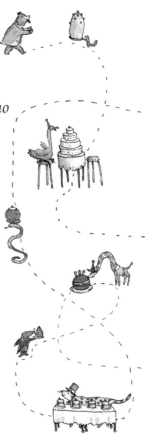

That afternoon everyone
had a birthday party
or an early birthday
party or celebrated
something else
or just baked
a cake anyway.
The bear ran from
one party to the
next until he couldn't
go any further.
Then he lay down
puffing and panting
under the willow,
and slowly fell
into a deep sleep
in the light of
the setting sun.

81

Dear Table

The squirrel sat in his house at the top of the beech tree. It was raining and it was winter. Gusty winds blew against his window. The ant was away on a journey.

The squirrel leaned on his table and said, with a deep sigh, and without meaning anything in particular, "There we go."

The table squeaked. It was a soft and ordinary sound, but it sounded as if the table wanted to say something back. The squirrel heard, "Oh . . . well . . ." They were slow and hesitant words from something that had always remained silent.

"I suppose I never really think about the table," the squirrel thought. "I never say anything to it, I never take it on a journey, never celebrate its birthday, never give it a gift, never ask what it fancies. It just stands there."

The squirrel sighed. "I suppose I should do something for it," he thought. "But what?"

He thought for a long time and then decided to write a letter to the table.

He took a piece of beech bark, put it on the table, and started writing:

Dear Table,
Is there anything I can do for you?

He put his pen down.

"What else can I write to the table?"
he wondered. "Is there something
I can tell it? I think it already knows
everything I do."

He thought deeply, but he couldn't
think of anything and finally wrote his
name in large letters at the bottom:

SQUIRREL

"For you," he said. He slid the
letter to the middle of the table.

The storm threw the window
open, grabbed the letter, and knocked
the table over with an enormous bang,
making it bounce up and down at
least five times. Then it slammed
the window shut again with a
deafening crash.

The squirrel sat in his chair, feeling
dazed. The table lay on its side in a
corner. The letter was gone.

After a while, the squirrel stood
up and righted the table. The drawer
was on the floor, and next to it, the
squirrel noticed a letter with curled
up corners that did not look familiar
to him. He opened it and read:

Dear Squirrel,

That wasn't falling, that was dancing.
For you, because you thought of me.
You don't have to do any more than
think of me.
Your dear table

The squirrel didn't wonder how
the table could have written the
letter. He rested his head on his
front paws, and his front paws on
the table, and fell asleep.

Rain

Dear Sparrow,

*It's raining, and do you know what?
It will never, ever stop raining. It will
keep raining forever. You just name
a day, Sparrow, as far away as possible.
On that day it will still be raining.
And the day after, too.*

I know it.

*Up until now the sun always
reappeared. But not any more.*

*You'll never see it again, Sparrow.
Nor will you see any dust for a bath.*

*There will only be mud and slush.
Just you watch.*

*Have you ever heard
of buckets?*

That's the way it will keep raining,
Sparrow—buckets.

And what's that I hear? Hissing?

Yes, because it's even raining
on the sun now, Sparrow. The sun
is going out, behind the clouds.
It's hissing. Right now, Sparrow.

Just watch out in case a wet,
round thing suddenly splashes down.

Watch out it doesn't fall and soak
your head. You, with your
carefree chirping, as if
it's all so natural!

The crow

Dear Crow,
I received your letter. Thanks a lot!
I let it dry first
and then I read it.
Very interesting!

It's always nice to hear from you.
I'm sorry to say that I briefly chirped
with pleasure as I read your letter.

If I look up, I can just see you sitting
there, did you know that? You're on the
bottom branch of the oak tree.

Your feathers are gleaming in the sun.

I think you squawk beautifully. Sadly,
but that's what makes it so beautiful.

The sparrow

The Memoirs

of the Ant

Dear Squirrel,

Today I want to write my memoirs.
The memoirs of the ant.

My first memory is of honey.
I was sailing a boat across
a sea of honey.

The ant put down his pen
and thought, "That's strange.
I don't remember that at all.

I'd better start remembering it,

then," he thought, and carried
on writing:

I reached a beach of sugar and
the giraffe was standing there.
He stooped low in front of me and put
me on a chair made of candied peel.

Animals approached from all sides (the rhino, the bear, the beetle, and you too, Squirrel, you may have forgotten, but you were there too), and called, "Ant! Ant!"

I nodded.

They put cakes and puddings in front of me.

The sun went down in front of my very eyes and the moon came up and it rained honey.

I gave a speech and everyone fell over with surprise (you too, Squirrel), and ran away to get more cakes, pudding, sugar, sweet nuts, jelly, and pies. They built a palace for me and I . . .

The ant remembered more and
more. He wrote for hours and hours,
until it was dark and he felt hungry.
The last sentence he wrote was,

> *This is part one of the*
> *memoirs of the ant.*
> *The ant*

"I suppose it's a book,
really," he thought,
"and so it's for everyone."

He threw his memoirs into
the air. The wind didn't know
what to do with them and blew
them in all directions.

They fell to earth far away, in the ocean, in the desert, in the snow, at the North Pole, and on the moon and stars.

Meanwhile, the ant was sitting at home, frowning at his last grain of sugar. It was so small he was scared to put it in his mouth. He was afraid he wouldn't taste a thing.

"To be an ant is so contradictory," he thought. He wasn't sure if it was true, but he considered it to be a nice thought and leaned backwards thoughtfully in his chair by his window.

All the Animals Wrote

When will I get some mail?"
the sparrow wondered.
"No one thinks of me."

He sat on the grass
under the linden tree,
chirping somberly. It was a beautiful day.
Suddenly he had an idea.
"I'll teach letter writing,"
he thought.
"That's what I'll do!"

He spread his wings and flew
across the woods and the river and
along the beach, inviting everyone
who wanted to write letters to take
lessons from him.

The next day, numerous animals who wanted to write a letter more than anything gathered in the clearing in the middle of the woods: the beetle, the kingfisher, the hoopoe, and even the iguana.

Everyone was given a pen and a piece of beech bark.

"Let's start," said the sparrow, and he jumped up and down in front of the class. His pupils held their pens firmly and listened attentively.

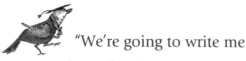 "We're going to write me
a letter," said the sparrow.

"'Dear Sparrow'. Write that down."

All the animals leaned forward
and slowly and carefully wrote:
Dear Sparrow.

The sparrow cleared his throat and
continued, "Write underneath:
'How are you?'"

All the animals wrote:
How are you?

"That is such a beautiful question,"
said the sparrow. "You should never,
ever forget that. Not in a single letter.
And underneath you should write . . ."

The sparrow stopped briefly.

"Oh dear," he thought. He scratched behind his ear with a wingtip. Then he said, "'Shall I bake a cake for you?' Yes. Write that down. That's a beautiful sentence. 'Shall I bake a cake for you?' You have to go easy on a sentence like that. And then, underneath, 'I'll bring it round later.' Write that down."

The animals wrote:

Shall I bake a cake for you?
I'll bring it round later.

"And at the bottom, write your name," said the sparrow.

He jumped up and down, feeling satisfied.

Then he stood still.

"But," he said, "you must never write anything untrue in a letter. So when you write that you're going to bake a cake for someone, then you really have to do it. And if you write that you're going to bring it round later, you really do have to bring it round later."

The animals nodded diligently and did their best to remember everything as well as they could.

Then the sparrow showed the animals how to throw a letter in the air and explained that the wind always, always delivered it.

The animals threw their letters in the air, thanked the sparrow, and went home.

The sparrow fluttered slowly through the warm sunlight to his home at the foot of the linden tree. "That was a useful lesson," he thought.

He had only just got home
when all the letters were delivered.
Dozens of envelopes piled up.

The sparrow was buried beneath
them. "From my pupils," he said to himself
proudly.

Later that day, his pupils came round,
one by one, with the cakes they had promised
in their letters. There were too many for the
sparrow to eat on his own, so he shared
them with his pupils. It was a long, cheerful
summer evening.

By the time dusk fell,
there wasn't a crumb left.
The sparrow stood up and wrote, in
large letters in the sand:

Dear pupils,
Thank you very much.
Your master, the sparrow

"Look," he said. "That's a thank-you
letter." The animals nodded. Then they
went home, filled with admiration for
the sparrow.

Balance

$\mathcal{D}$ear Squirrel,

If you don't mind, then I'd like to make a short speech at your birthday party.

You see, I've discovered something called balance.

Have you ever heard of it?

Balance, that's what it's called.

I'm convinced that everyone will find it very interesting.

I would like to make my speech from the top of the beech tree, with everyone below me on the ground.

(I won't make it too long.)

The elephant

Dear Elephant,

Of course you can make a speech. But I'd rather you made it from the special chair I made for you, a chair that will stand at the head of the table. Otherwise, some animals won't be able to hear you, and that would be a pity.

The squirrel

Dear Squirrel,

No, no. It has to be from the top of the beech tree. I want to illustrate my words and you can't illustrate while sitting in a chair.

I'll shout loudly and lean forward as far as I can. If you make sure people are standing right underneath me, then everyone will hear.

Oh, Squirrel, this balance thing is fascinating!

The elephant

The Bear and the Ant

The bear and the ant sat side by side at the rhino's party. There was a cake in front of them.

The bear pulled the cake toward him with a flourish and started eating. After a while, the ant asked, "May I have a piece too?" The bear took another bite of cake, looked at the ant, and tried to say something, but his mouth was too full. He took a piece of paper and wrote:

My mouth is too full.
What did you say?

"May I have a piece too?" said the ant, a little louder this time.

The bear continued to chew
and replied in writing:

*If you want to ask me anything,
you'll have to write it down. My jaws are
grinding deafeningly and I can't hear a
word you're saying.*

The ant picked up
a piece of paper and wrote:

May I have a piece too?

The bear took a giant bite,
reflected briefly, and then wrote:

A piece of what?

The ant started grinding his teeth
and wrote:

*May I have a piece of this cake
before it's finished?*

The bear put the last piece in his mouth and said, "Mmm, delicious."

Then he called out, "What kind of cake was that, Rhino?"

"Sweet grass cake," called the rhino.

"Oh," said the bear.

He turned to the ant in surprise.

"Didn't you want to try a piece?" he asked.

But the ant had risen to his feet and was standing somberly behind a branch of the willow, gazing at the ground. The bear sighed as his chair creaked, then snapped, and he slowly tumbled to the floor.

You May Not Fall Down

$\mathcal{Y}$ou know what?"
thought the elephant,
"if I were to put a note down
here, on the ground, so
I could read it from above,
then I would be just fine."
He rubbed his front paws together
and wrote in huge letters:

You may not fall down

Then he put the note under the
chestnut tree and began to climb.

He was halfway up the tree and
hidden among the leaves when the
cricket walked by. He read the note
on the ground.

"Oh," he thought. "At last!"
He had been searching for the word
"Not" for ages.

He already had "Nowhere" and
"None" and "Never" and "Nothing".
But he didn't have "Not".

He rubbed his antennae together,
looked around, saw the coast was
clear, and tore the word "Not" from
the elephant's note.

There was nothing he wanted
more than to hang the word on his
front door, in front of his name.
"Not the cricket," it would say. He would
chirp loudly inside the house and look
out through a crack in the wall at the
passers-by. "Not the cricket?" they
would say. "Not the cricket? So who's
chirping then?"

They would knock on the door and call, "Who's chirping?" He wouldn't say anything and wouldn't open the door and only chirp louder.

They would be bewildered. Bewilderment—the cricket loved that. Wrinkled brows, hesitation, and bewilderment.

He flew home cheerfully, with the word "Not" under one wing.

When the elephant finally reached the top of the chestnut tree, panting after his long climb, he wobbled and almost fell. But then he remembered the note.

"Oh yes," he thought, "it's a good thing too."

He looked down to the ground. "What?" he cried in surprise.

He read the words three times.
"But I may *not* fall!" he said.
He teetered and tottered.
"So I may fall," he thought
stoically, and with an enormous
noise, he tumbled down from
the top of the tree.
The squirrel found the
elephant a little later with
the note beside him.
He carefully straightened his
bruised and battered trunk.
The elephant looked up and groaned.
"I'll never understand anything
ever again, Squirrel."
"No," said the squirrel and he sat
down in the grass beside him.

127

Ant

*O*ne morning, the squirrel sat at his table and decided to write a letter to the ant. He didn't know how he should write what he wanted to write. *Hello, Ant,* he began.

But that wasn't what he meant. He put the letter on the floor and started again. *Dear Ant,* he wrote. But that looked even less apt. At the top of a new sheet, he wrote,

Hi, Ant, and on top of the next, *Ant!* And then, *Ant,* and, *Oh, Ant,* and, *Amiable Ant,* and, *Ant, Ant . . .* He kept on all morning, sighing more and more deeply as time passed. "There has to be a beginning," he thought, "that ideally suits the ant." He was certain there was, but he couldn't come up with it. The pile of letters on the floor around the squirrel got larger and larger. Finally, the squirrel stood up, waded through the letters, and opened his door to sit on the branch in front of his house and think.

But when he stepped outside, the wind slipped in, tore the letters from his room, and blew them in a little whirlwind all the way to the ant.

It was a beautiful day and the ant was sitting in the sun outside his house, thinking about the distance. Suddenly, he was buried in swirling letters.

They tumbled down into piles that reached far above his head. With difficulty, he wormed his way out of the gigantic pile and started reading.

By the time he had finished, it was late in the evening and the moon had risen. The ant sat still briefly and looked at the bushes in the dark.

Then he carefully piled up the letters until they reached all the way up to the edge of his roof. Then he climbed up the side of his house, lay down, pulled the letter that said, 'Dear Ant' over him like a blanket, and fell asleep. The moon shone and when the ant turned over, the letters rustled. The ant nodded in his sleep and murmured, "The ant, that's me."

The Cricket's Note

One day, the cricket
wrote a note:

   I'm out.

He hung it on his door and was gone.
When he returned, he was just in time
to see the note fly away.

   "That's strange," he thought.
"I really was out." He had no idea
where he had been.

   Then he wrote:

I'll be in the desert for a while.

And he strolled into the middle
of the desert.
"How strange. How strange!" he thought.

   When he returned a while later, he
thought deeply and then wrote:

Here is an enormous cake.

He found himself sitting in front
of an enormous cake.
"So everything I write happens!"
he thought. He opened his mouth,
but before he could take a single
bite, a passer-by, who looked
strikingly like the bear, had
already eaten the
whole cake.

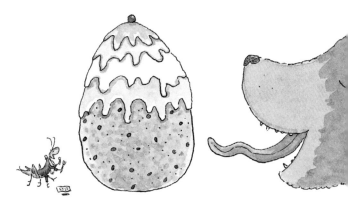

137

So the cricket wrote:

Only me, the cricket, will eat the cake now standing in front of me.

Just to make sure, he wrote underneath:

No one else.

Suddenly a cake was standing

before him, and he ate it all on his own. But it wasn't very tasty and he didn't enjoy it at all.

"Now I don't feel like anything anymore," he thought. He had never had that thought before.

He looked somberly at the floor
and thought, "All I can do now is chirp."

He started chirping but his song
sounded melancholy and out of tune.

He thought briefly and wrote:

*I always chirp cheerfully
and tunefully.*

And he chirped cheerfully
and tunefully all day long.

There was no end to his chirping.

By evening he found
he was almost crying,
yet he was still
chirping and it
was still cheerful
and tuneful.

Then the cricket wrote that he was
not going to write any more notes and he
didn't hang anything else on his door.

"Letters are dangerous,"
he thought to himself.

In his thoughts he saw letters with
antlers storming toward him; letters
with spines and letters with very sharp
teeth. He crawled into a corner of his
house, terrified.

"I'm only thinking that!" he cried.
"I didn't write it down!"

All the notes disappeared from his thoughts and he was on his own.

In silence, in the moonlight, he baked a very small, very friendly cake, and ate it slowly and cautiously.

The Elephant

(at Sea)

One day, the elephant built himself a raft and sailed out to sea. The carp, the pike, the bream, and the salmon swam along behind him.

Everyone knew it: the elephant was going to sea. On his raft, without a mast, he was going to live at sea.

"It's the only way," he had said to everyone, and everyone had nodded. It was the only way to stop him climbing on everything and falling off again.

"Is there really nothing at sea?" he had asked the animals who knew about the sea.

"No, nothing at all," they had said.

"Not even one tree? One tree
standing there accidentally?"

"No."

The elephant had sighed deeply
and wiped a couple of heavy tears
from his cheeks.

He packed a chest of sweet beechnuts
to take with him. Then the thrush taught
him to whistle so he had something to do
while he floated along.

The beach was crowded with animals
who had come to see him off.

"Goodbye, Elephant!" they called.

They shouted, waved, and climbed
on each other's shoulders.

"Goodbye, everyone,"
said the elephant.

The gull flew high above him and
the frog jumped in the water and tried
to swim over to him.

"One final farewell!" he croaked.

"Goodbye, Frog," said the elephant.

The squirrel climbed onto his roof
and raised his lamp high above his head
so the elephant could see him one last
time. The lamp sparkled in the sunlight.

"Elephant!" called the squirrel.
"Elephant!"

The elephant looked and saw
the lamp.

"Goodbye, Squirrel!" he called.

By evening, he had drifted far out to sea.

The animals heard no more from the elephant. Some forgot him or thought he had never existed. Others missed him and thought about him every day.

Some time later, on the morning of his birthday, the squirrel received a letter from the elephant:

Dear Squirrel,

Happy birthday.

Are you still living in the beech tree, right up near the top?

Do you still have that lamp?

                    The elephant (at sea)

That evening, as he celebrated his birthday, the squirrel missed the elephant more than anyone or anything. Briefly, very briefly, he thought he could see him far away, beyond the woods, among the stars, waving and calling, "Here I am!" just before he fell.

But that was impossible.
The squirrel knew that.

He sighed and continued to celebrate his birthday.

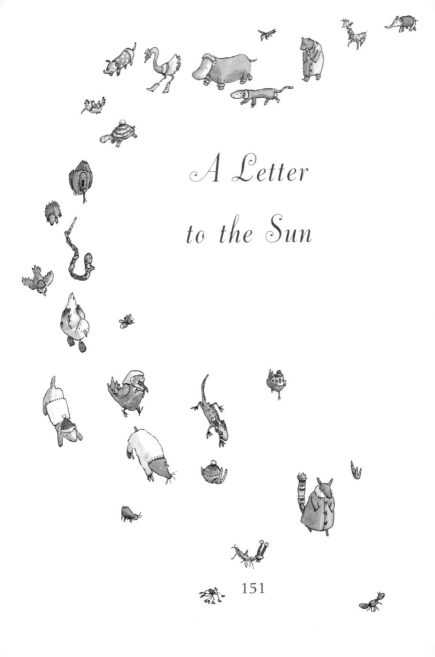

A Letter
to the Sun

On the very last day of the year,
when it was cold and dark in the woods,
the animals wrote a letter to the sun.

They thought at length about what
they should write and chose the most
cautious words they knew.

"It's a begging letter," said the ant.
"A cordial begging letter."

Almost all the animals signed their
names at the bottom of the letter.
Only the mole, the earthworm, the
moth, and the bat had their doubts.
They would have preferred to have
written to the moon.

Hundreds of animals gathered together and threw the letter upward. The icy wind blew it into the sky, straight through the low-hanging clouds.

Shivering, they sat together, waiting for an answer. As they waited they blew on their antennae and wrapped their wings around each other for warmth.

Toward the end of the afternoon,
a small hole suddenly appeared
in the clouds. A ray of sunlight shot
through and a letter drifted down.

The animals looked on, wide-eyed.
The letter landed on the ground
and the ant stepped forward to
open it. The slug leaned on the
hippopotamus's shoulder,
the spider leaned on the
hedgehog's shoulder,
and together
they read:

Dear animals,
That's fine. See you soon.
The sun

The animals breathed a sigh of relief, nodded at each other, shook each other's wings, fins, antennae, and paws, wished each other all the very best, and went home.

That evening, most of the animals danced a few steps while quietly singing,

"See you soon, see you soon . . ."

Then they climbed into bed and fell asleep.

About the Author

$\mathcal{T}$oon Tellegen is one of
Holland's most celebrated writers
for both children and adults. He
started his literary career as a poet
and began writing for children
in the mid 1980s. Toon lives in
Amsterdam, and loves reading,
telling stories, and huge, sweet cakes.

About the Illustrator

*J*essica Ahlberg studied at Winchester School of Art and has gone on to illustrate several books for children. She likes, among other things, writing letters, looking at maps, reading books, doing home improvements, and making cakes. She lives in Brighton, England, and loves walking by the ocean and sometimes swimming in it.

*R*ead about another book
from Toon Tellegen . . .

The Squirrel's Birthday and Other Parties

"That evening, the animals made their
gifts for the squirrel. They did so quietly and
underwater, or deep in the bushes, or high
above the clouds, because they wanted to
surprise the squirrel. Everyone made a gift.
The world rustled and shook, but very quietly,
so that the squirrel, sitting in the dark by his
window, thought it was so silent everywhere
that he could only hear his heart beating."

Toon Tellegen's whimsical tales are perfectly
complemented by Jessica Ahlberg's delicate
illustrations in this collection of lyrical stories
that will captivate readers of all ages.

For David, Pat, and Phoebe
Toon Tellegen

For Saskia
Jessica Ahlberg

First American edition published in 2009
by Boxer Books Limited.

Distributed in the United States and Canada by
Sterling Publishing Co., Inc.
387 Park Avenue South, New York, NY 10016-8810

First published in Great Britain in 2009
by Boxer Books Limited.
www.boxerbooks.com

Copyright © 1996 by Toon Tellegen, Amsterdam,
Em. Querido's Uitgeverij B.V.

Text copyright © 1996 Toon Tellegen
Illustrations copyright © 2009 Jessica Ahlberg

Translated by Martin Cleaver

Edited by Frances Elks

Original English translation copyright © 2009 Boxer Books Limited

Book design by Amelia Edwards

The rights of Toon Tellegen to be identified as the author and
Jessica Ahlberg as the illustrator of this work have been asserted by
them in accordance with the Copyright, Designs and Patents Act, 1988.

ISBN 978-1-906250-95-9

1 3 5 7 9 10 8 6 4 2

Printed in Italy

All of our papers are sourced from managed forests
and renewable resources.